The Adventures of Farad J.

Written by Farad J. Mills
Category: Children's Fiction
Edition: First
Illustrations inspired by: Winfred Thorpe
Copyright © 2018 by Stephanie Mills

ISBN 978-0-359-25280-0

Edited by: Pam McNeil
Illustration Layout/Page Layout/Graphic Art:
Bobby Ray Ivory Jr/IvoryCoast Media

Foreword

In first grade, I met an unlikely friend, one who is mentally and physically different from me. His name is Farad Mills, and he has Down Syndrome. Farad and I have been friends for over ten years, to the point where I consider him family, and he too looks up to me as an older brother. Farad is a fantastic individual who can light up a room with his smile, and he changed my life forever.

Farad taught me patience, compassion, and the meaning of unconditional friendship. Though I have never treated him differently, I always try to make sure he knows just how extraordinary he is. Having a friend with Farad's disorder taught me how to embrace diversity, how to treat people and to slow down and not be so dangerous all the time. Due to his condition, he has the mindset of a child which means that he still has a beautiful outlook on the world and is always amazed when learning something new. Farad sees no evil and takes life day by day. I try to implement his perspective on living every day though it can be challenging at times. Our friendship has taught me that diversity is much broader than race, it encompasses so much more. Interactions with people different from ourselves increase our knowledge base. Research shows that we learn more from people who are different from us than we do from people who are similar to us. The more diverse perspectives found in the classroom and throughout campus, the more productive the discussions will be and the more creative we will become. Learning to work with students with different thoughts, ideas, beliefs, and even disabilities will only help prepare me to succeed in our increasingly diverse workforce. Additionally, diversity enhances our self-awareness. By being more self-aware, we are more capable of making informed decisions about our academic and professional future. I will forever be grateful that Farad came into my life. I know that I've gained more from being his friend then he has learned from me, and I will never take that for granted.

Sincerely,

Kevin Frazier

Acknowledgement

Farad J. Mills is my beautiful young man. He's the most creative, loving, compassionate human being that I know. I'm so thankful that God blessed me with him.

Your Mom,

Stephanie Mills

Dedication

Dedicated to the memory of

Joe T. Mills and Christine Mills,

my beloved grandparents

FARAD AND SHANICE VISIT ...

It is winter and I decided that it was a good time to take a trip. Shanice and I decided that New York would be a fun place to visit because we both loved New York! I wanted to go there to hang out with my friends Shelby and Sid. Shanice and I called our friend Emma to invite her along too, and she said yes. I was really excited because I love New York. It is so exciting and there are a lot of things to do there.

When we got to New York, we met Shelby and Sid at the airport. They lived in New York and the last time that I had seen them was on my 15th birthday. Shelby and Sid were 15 years old, and they had come to hang out with me on my birthday last year. I remember us having a great time; especially playing tug of war at the hotel. Since Shanice was unable to come with me on last year's trip, I wasn't able to use my rope for pranks. So, I decided to use the rope for tug of war. I brought the rope along on this trip because I wanted to use it in some pranks this time, and also to play another game of tug of war. It would be fun playing with so many people this time.

When we got to the hotel, we all put our suitcases away. After that, we decided where everyone would sleep, and I shouted, "The first thing that we are going to do is have some contests! Let's start with tug of war."

Emma said, "Cool, and I'm going to win!"

"I don't think so," I said. "Shanice, you'll be on my team and we're going to pull against Emma's team. Shelby and Sid will be on Emma's team.

I got my rope from my bag and put it in the middle of the floor. Each team took hold of each end. We all started to pull hard. Shanice and I were pulling harder. I got tired because it was three of them against us two, but I kept on pulling. My hands were starting to hurt. I was pulling so hard that I could hear my bones popping. I could even see my muscles getting bigger through my shirt. When this happened, I became super strong! I helped us win that round.

After we won, I said, "Emma's team are the losers."

"We're so tired," Emma replied, "but we will challenge you guys to another round."

We played a second round, and Emma, Shelby, and Sid beat us that time. We continued to play games in the hotel room and ended up messing the room up pretty badly.

"The next game that we play will be called chores," I said. I suggested that we play chores in order to get the room clean again.

I said, "Whoever gets their chores done first gets to watch whatever show they want to see on t.v."

Emma and I made up the bed. Shelby and Sid put things back in the suitcases and then put all of the suitcases out of sight. Shanice cleaned off all of the furniture by throwing away the trash that was left from our snacks and drinks. I won the game of chores because I got my side of the room finished first. So, I chose what we would all watch on the large screen TV.

"We're going to watch the Carolina Panthers play football because I love to watch Cam Newton play. He's my favorite quarterback," I told them.

No one was excited about my choice, and they all ended up falling asleep. I tried to watch all of the game, but I ended up falling asleep too. This was because we were all so tired from the games. After about an hour, Shanice woke up and then woke me up. She kissed me on my cheek and said thanks for suggesting that we travel to New York. She told me that she was having a great time and asked me if I wanted to go downstairs to take a walk. I said yes, but when we left out of the room, the sound of the door closing woke up the other girls. When we got off of the elevator, we looked back and saw the other girls getting off another elevator. Once I saw the girls coming off the elevator, I looked at Shanice and whispered, "Let's run!"

Shanice and I started to run as fast as we could because we wanted to get the girls to chase us in a game of tag. We ran into the street, and I almost got hit by a car. I looked up and saw a red light and stopped just in time. Shanice and I decided that we had not made the best choice.

"This isn't a good idea," Shanice said. "Playing in the streets is dangerous."

"You're right," I said. "Hey, I know what we can do!" I yelled. "We can go to the movies!"

At the movies, I decided that it was time to prank someone. So, I decided to prank Emma. On the way to the movies, I had stopped to pick up some leftover snow that was on the ground. It had snowed a couple of days before we got to New York and because it was so cold, all of it had not melted. While Emma was watching the movie and not paying any attention to me, I took the snow from my jacket pocket. I whispered Emma's name and when she looked over at me, I took the some snow and placed it in each of my hands and smashed it in her face. The snow melted against her warm face - it even got in her eyes. Emma could not see the movie because she had cold water from the snow in her eyes. I laughed so hard! Seeing her with her eyes closed and the white snow melting down her face was the funniest sight ever!

Luckily, Emma had tissues in her coat pocket. She used her tissues to clean her eyes. Emma also had powders in her coat pocket. So, while I was still laughing really hard, Emma pulled out the powders and poured some into her hands. She took her hands and wiped the powders all over my face and glasses. Some of the powders ended up getting into my eyes. I closed my eyes and tried to wipe away the powders, but I couldn't. So, I decided to get up to go to the bathroom to put water in my eyes. I was still rubbing my eyes when I got up, and walked past Shanice, I accidentally stepped on her silver high-heeled shoes. Shanice got really angry at me because those are her favorite shoes. She also got angry at me for interrupting the movie. She looked at me with an angry face and she started to breathe really hard. She was so upset that she got up from her seat to step on my new shoes. This made me really angry and caused me to breathe really hard too. We both stared at each other for a long time. She didn't stop staring me down and I refused to stop staring her down with angry eyes and eyes that were still burning from the powders. As she continued to stare me down, she decided to fold her arms to show me just how angry she was. So, I folded my arms too. Neither one of us would break the stare. Emma, Shelby and Sid were watching the whole time. Then, Shanice called me stupid for bringing the snow into the movie in the first place. I then called her a jerk for calling me names first.

We returned to our seats to finish watching the movie and we refused to look each other's way. When the movie ended, we refused to speak to each other. Then, I started to feel sad because I had not apologized to Emma or Shanice. I do not like it when my friends and I are mad at each other. So, I went over to Emma and Shanice and gave them a hug.

They each hugged me back, and Shelby and Sid joined in for a group hug. We all apologized. We were able to catch another movie which was a comedy and we laughed and enjoyed each other the rest of the evening and the rest of our time in New York.

LESSON LEARNED: PRANKS CAN CAUSE PROBLEMS BETWEEN FRIENDS!

MADDIE SAVES FARAD FROM THE WEREWOLF

After the prank that caused the building to catch fire, Shanice decided that we should take a break from playing pranks on people. She said that the prank with the fire shooting gas trumpet had gone way too far. She was right about that. I learned that using fire in pranks is too dangerous and I would never do that again, but I still felt that playing harmless pranks wouldn't hurt anybody. Shanice did not think so. She said that the whole fire experience had frightened her and she felt that my stay in the hospital should have me thinking about chilling out for a while. I did chill for a couple of days after my hospital stay, but now I was ready for some fun!

I was really starting to get bored, so I picked up the phone and called up Maddie to see if she wanted to come and hang out with me. I also wanted to see if she and I could come up with some new ideas for pranks.

"Hey Maddie, would you like to come over to hang out with me?"

"Sure, I can come right over."

"Great! I was thinking that you can come over and we come up with some new ways to prank people."

"We're the pranksters, right?" she asked.

"Yep. So, let's get ready to have some fun!" I said.

"I love playing pranks and having fun!" she said.

"While we're planning new pranks, we could also play some games," I told her.

"That sounds fun. I'm on my way," she said.

When Maddie got to my house we decided to play board games. We also played air hockey. We were having a really good time. We were having so much fun playing the games they we forgot all about pranks. We didn't even notice that the sky had turned dark and there was a thunderstorm coming--What we heard next, sounded like a gunshot.

"Crash! Bang!" The sound of that thunder was even louder than a gunshot! Then the rain started to come down. It came down so hard that it was even coming in through the open window of my game room. I had to put the window down to keep it from coming inside. The storm was really bad. The thunder and lightning caused the lights to go out.

Maddie and I looked at each other because we didn't know what to do next. My Mom wasn't home and the weather was too bad for Maddie to leave, so we just stood there in the dark. As we were standing, trying to figure out what to do, we heard a spooky sound coming from my mom's bedroom.

I listened really hard and that's when I realized that the sound was coming from a werewolf. It must have snuck into the house when my mom left the door cracked as she unloaded the food from the car. The werewolf had been so quiet because he wanted to wait until my mom was gone before he tried to attack me.

Maddie and I crept closer to my mom's room to see where the werewolf was. We were really afraid because he sounded really angry.

We were walking down the hall and that's when the lights came back on. This was good because at least we'd be able to see the werewolf now.

When we got to my mom's bedroom, we saw the werewolf hiding in her closet. Her closet was a good place for the werewolf to hide because she has so much stuff in there. As I got closer to the werewolf, I could see that he had my red iPad!

"How dare he?" I thought to myself. I have to get my iPad back, but how? Then, I remembered that Maddie had special powers. She shared this with me when we were talking and playing games. So, I asked Maddie to use her special powers to turn me into a werewolf. Who knew that I'd end up playing a prank on a werewolf! I needed to prank the werewolf by making him think that I was a real werewolf. If he thought that I was also a werewolf, maybe he would let my iPad go.

Maddie wasn't sure if this was a good idea, but she used her powers anyway. Once she turned me into a werewolf, I was scared and excited all at the same time. I was scared because this werewolf looked so angry, but I was also excited to get up close to a real werewolf because everyone knows how much I LOVE werewolves!

So, I went up to the werewolf to try to get my iPad. As I reached out my finger to try and drag it closer to me with one of my long claws, he bit me. This angry werewolf was not going to play nice. He growled at me and looked as if he was going to bite me again. I was so scared, but I did not want him to destroy my iPad. I wanted to run, but I knew that the werewolf would chase me. I felt helpless.

That is when Maddie came to my rescue. She used her special powers again. She used a spell to help me get rid of the werewolf. Maddie twirled her fingers around and then pointed one of them at the werewolf. When she did this, he didn't look so mean anymore, so I growled at him. Once I saw that he was now afraid of me, I growled at him again with the longest, scariest growl that I could let out—the one that sounds like a chainsaw.

When I let out this terrible growl, the werewolf growled back at me. This time, I wasn't afraid. I howled and then jumped on the werewolf before he could think about jumping on me.

I bit him on one of his long fangs. I bit on it so hard that I ended up yanking the tooth out! The werewolf could not believe that I pulled his longest fang out of his mouth. He just stood there looking at the tooth hanging from my mouth. After that, all he could do was walk away.

I felt relieved and happy. I was able to get my iPad back, and I survived a fight with a werewolf.

But I knew that I had to give Maddie all of the credit. She was the one that used her special powers to help me to defeat the werewolf.

"Thank you," I said to Maddie.

"You're welcome," she said.

"Can I have a hug?" I asked.

"Sure," she said.

I gave her a hug and I told her that I loved hanging out with her and she smiled.

"So, now that the lights are back on, do you want to finish this game of air hockey? You may have defeated the werewolf, but you won't defeat me in the game," Maddie said.

"I bet you I will," I said.

"I bet you won't," she said.

"We'll see about that!" I told her.

So, we continued to have fun playing games and laughing. We had so much fun that I forgot that we were supposed to come up with ideas on how to prank people.

When my mom came home, we told her all about the storm and the lights going out, and the werewolf. She thought that it was funny. I don't know if she believed me.

"You guys are too much," she said.

"No, the werewolf was too much!" Maddie and I both said at the same time.

LESSON LEARNED: DON'T PLAY PRANKS ON WILD ANIMALS! GETTING BIT BY A WEREWOLF HURTS!

THE GAS TRUMPET

" I have an idea for our next prank," I said to Shanice.

"What is it this time?" She asked.

"I want to prank the band members with a fire-shooting gas trumpet at practice today."

"I don't know about that, Farad."

"Well, I know so," I said.

"Have you really thought about this one? Maybe we should take a break from the pranks."

"We are going to do more pranks. You know how much fun it is to get a good laugh!"

" I love doing pranks too. But you're talking about using a fire-shooting gas trumpet? Don't you even think about it," Shanice told me.

"I've already thought about it," I said.

We continued to argue about it until it was time for me to get ready for band practice.

I got dressed and grabbed the trumpet. Shanice joined me, but she was still mad. Then, it seemed like the trumpet started to talk to me. It sounded like it said, "stop that pranking!"

I didn't listen to Shanice. I didn't listen to the voice coming from the trumpet either. I was feeling too excited to listen to anybody. I felt that this was one of my best pranks ever and I couldn't wait to use it!

When we got to the football field, everyone was already there and ready to begin practice. We were practicing for a big band competition. Everybody was going to be surprised because they didn't know that I had switched trumpets.

We all got in line and everyone began to play their instruments. As they played their music, I began to blow into the fire-shooting gas trumpet. When I blew into it, fire shot out and it went everywhere!

I started to think to myself, how did the fire get to be so big?' When I practiced it earlier, there was only a little fire that came out. But this fire was huge. It went in the direction of the cheerleaders and they all ran away screaming. The fire was so big that it reached the school building. The fire caused the building to start burning.

I started to think about the people on the inside and so I ran in to rescue them. I was able to get everyone out of the building safely, but I got a burn spot on my uniform. The spark of fire burned through my uniform and caused me to get a little burn on my skin. After the fire department came to put out the fire, I had to be taken to the hospital to get the small burn taken care of.

While I was in the hospital, my Mom came to see me. She was happy to know that I was OK, but she was angry about the dangerous prank that I decided to play. She told me that she would have to ground me for making such a bad decision when I got out of the hospital, and I understood. When she left, I asked her to take my band uniform to the seamstress to get it fixed. I loved my uniform. I know that I was going to be alright. I just wanted to make sure that it was going to be alright too.

The fire had burned a hole in my uniform, but my hat didn't get messed up at all. As I ran through the building to warn people to get out, my hat never fell off of my head either. I was so happy about to see that my hat was OK because I LOVE my band hat!!

When Shanice came to visit, I told her that I was doing fine and showed her my hat. I told her that my hat was awesome.

"What do you mean by that?" she asked.

"See," I said as I showed her the hat. "It didn't get any fire burns and it protected my hair and my head from the fire. That's why it's awesome."

"I see," Shanice said. " And I see that you're still handsome."

I just smiled. Sometimes I wished that Shanice was my girlfriend.

Shanice started to look around the room. She saw my trumpet near the closet and thought that it was the fire-shooting gas trumpet.

"NO MORE PRANKS!" she said.

"Yes," I said. "More pranks!"

Shanice glared at me.

"But, no more pranks with fire," I told her. "Don't worry-I have destroyed the fire-shooting gas trumpet. Over there is my original band trumpet, and I am going to play it for you. So, what do you want to hear?

"Can you play Uptown Funk by Bruno Mars?" she asked.

"I sure can," I said.

Shanice went over to get the trumpet for me. I took it and started to play, and Shanice started to dance. We were having a good time and then the phone rang. It was my friend Maddie calling to see how I was doing.

She was also calling to find out how the fire started. I told her that I was fine, but that I had gotten expelled from school for causing the fire.

"Oh, no!" Maddie said.

"It's alright," I said. "I made a bad choice, but I've learned my lesson. I will never use fire in a prank again."

"I'm glad that you're Okay," she said. "So does that mean that you won't be pulling anymore pranks on people?"

"No more pranks!" I said. "Gotcha!" I yelled after that.

"I knew that you were joking," she said.

"You know that I'm a prankster, Maddie and I love to do pranks. I'll just make them safer the next time."

"I'm a prankster, too!" Maddie shared.

"Hey, maybe we can do some pranks together!" I yelled out.

"Oh, no!" Shanice yelled from the background. "Not another prankster!"

"Yes!" I said. "Maddie will be the perfect person to give us new ideas for some pranks."

All Shanice could do was shake her head. I told Maddie goodbye and hung up the phone. I got up from my hospital bed so that I could play the trumpet and dance. I was feeling good because I would be able to soon start playing some new pranks on people.

As I danced, Shanice sat in the corner, shaking her head—"No…not now. No more pranks…"

I just laughed because I couldn't wait for Maddie to give us some fresh ideas.

LESSON LEARNED: WHEN PLAYING PRANKS, DON'T EVER PLAY WITH FIRE!

THE HAUNTED HOUSE

" I will be dressing as a werewolf for Halloween this year," I said.

" You're so weird," Shanice replied. "All you think about is werewolves."

" I'm not weird, but my costume is," I joked.

"You're funny," Shanice said.

" I know. That's why you like me so much, right? "

" Yeah, sure…whatever."

"When we go to the Halloween festival, I want to scare EVERYBODY this year, even Maddie."

" But, I thought that you were on punishment and couldn't go to the festival this year," Shanice said.

"This punishment is way too long," I said. "I am going to the festival anyway."

"I hope that you don't get into bigger trouble, Farad."

"I am not worried about that. I just want to go have some FUN!"

"Are you sure that you should go?" Shanice asked.

"Let's go," I said.

I put on my mask and Shanice and I headed out the door. We decided to walk since the Festival was only a 15 minute walk from my house.

Once we got to the festival, we bought our tickets and headed on in. I was excited because I couldn't wait to scare everybody with my biggest, scariest growl. I had been practicing it all week. I learned to be so great at growling by watching a lot of werewolf movies.

As we walked around the festival, I began to howl, "ooooowwwwoohhhhh!" When the people heard me, they began to run every which way. I just laughed because that wasn't even my biggest one. After that, I growled with the scariest, loudest growl I'd ever let out, "UUURRRGGGGHHHHHH!!" I did it twice. That's when everyone really started to run. Shanice laughed and said, "that was a GOOD one!"

We continued to walk through the park having fun and scaring people. When I looked up ahead, I saw Maddie.

"Hey Shanice, here comes Maddie. When she comes over, I am going to let out my scariest growl, the one that I just did, and scare her too."

"Hey, Maddie. Over here!" Shanice shouted as she waved for her to join us. Instead of saying 'hi' to Maddie, I growled the fiercest growl that I could. This one was even scarier than the one that I'd let out before. This one sounded like a chain saw, "AAAAARRRRRRRRGGGGGGGG!"

Maddie became so frightened that she started to run away.

"Don't go," I yelled. "It's just me."

When she heard my voice, she stopped in her tracks and started laughing. " You're such a prankster," Maddie said.

"Since we're all together, let's go have some fun," Shanice said. "How 'bout we go check out the haunted house?"

"Cool!" I said.

We walked to the part of the festival where the haunted house was. When we saw it, it looked very spooky. There were ghosts floating around the windows. It was old, and had old broken pieces of wood falling off of it. And you could hear ghost sounds coming from the inside.

When we got to the haunted house, Maddie went in first. I followed her and Shanice was behind me. Once we got inside, a vampire who was wearing a long, black cape and who had sharp, bloody teeth jumped out and bit Maddie on her arm. Shanice and I were so scared. We were watching Maddie to see what she was going to do. We thought that she would scream, but instead of screaming, she began to turn into a vampire too. And now she didn't fear the vampire at all. She partnered up with the vampire in the haunted house and began to scare the people who came inside.

Shanice and I started to run, but as we ran through the haunted house, we bumped into a witch. The witch had been hiding in a corner, but she jumped out and used her finger to put a spell on Shanice. Shanice was frozen in place. As Shanice stood unable to move, the witch, said in a spooky voice, "make her into a witch." She was turning Shanice into a witch! Shanice's outfit didn't change-she was still wearing her red jacket and white and red shirt. But now she was wearing silver shoes and a witch's hat. And now, when Shanice laughed, she sounded the same way that the witch did. Then, like Maddie, Shanice forgot about escaping, and joined up with the witch to frighten everyone.

Now, I was all alone in the haunted house, and feeling really scared. I wanted to get away from all of the madness. I was looking around to see how I could escape the madness and that's when a very angry looking werewolf appeared out of the darkness. I just stood there, not knowing what to do. I started to run, but before I could even think about it, he jumped on me and bit me.

After he bit me, I started to grow hair all over my body-just like a real werewolf. And just like Maddie and Shanice, I turned into the creature that attacked me. I forgot about escaping and joined up with the werewolf to scare people who came into the haunted house. Maddie, Shanice and I were now stuck in the haunted house forever....

One Halloween, my Mom and her friend Ms. Faye came to the haunted house. I was looking really spooky and my Mom didn't even recognize me, at first. But when I saw her, I started to have feelings again. The first thing I wanted to do was hug her. So I went up to her and said, "I love you."

"That's Farad!" My mom said. "I love you, too and I've missed you!"

When I heard those words, I magically turned back into myself. Once the spell was finally broken from me, Shanice and Maddie also turned back into their original selves.

"Let's get some ice cream, everybody!" I yelled.

"Yes! Let's get ice cream!" everyone agreed.

Everyone was so happy to be back to themselves that we forgot about the monsters. Maddie stopped cheering for ice cream when she heard something going, "breh, bru ,breh…breh, bru, breh. She looked up and there was the vampire.

We all screamed and ran to the door. That's when I heard a chainsaw sound, and when I looked back, it was the werewolf coming my way.

When Shanice looked back, she saw the witch coming toward her. All of the monsters were upset because we were no longer their partners.

My Mom opened the door so that we could escape. But before she let us out she said, "Farad, finish your punishment or be stuck here with the monsters again?

"Punishment!" I yelled. I thought that she had forgotten, but she had not. Then my Mom opened the door wide to let us all run through and Ms. Faye closed it tight. They didn't have to worry about the monsters attacking them, because they only wanted us.

LESSON LEARNED: PARENTS ARE SERIOUS ABOUT PUNISHMENTS AND THEY DON'T FORGET THEM EITHER!

THE TALKING DRUM

"Shanice, have you ever heard of a drum called the talking drum?"

"No, I haven't. What is it?

"It is a drum that is made in Africa that can talk. I learned about it from my teacher when we were studying drums. The talking drum is used by the African people to communicate between villages."

"Wow! So how does it work?"

"When you hit the drum in a different place, it can make a different sound. The different beats sound just like someone talking. The drum is used in battle to communicate between villages."

"That sounds neat. I'd love to see one."

"Do you really want to see one?

"Of course, I do!'

"Guess what? I have two of them."

"Are you serious?" Shanice asked.

"Yes. I asked my mom to get me one and she got me two of them."

"Where did she get them from?" asked Shanice.

"She got them from the American People village."

"That's so cool! Can I see them?"

"Sure," I said. "I want you to play one of the drums with me at the music festival today."

"Are you sure that you want me to play it?" Shanice asked.

"Let's play drums," I said.

"Can we practice first?" Shanice asked.

"We don't need to practice, Shanice, because we're not going to really 'play' the drums. This festival will be the perfect place for us to play one of our pranks and I want us to use the drums in our prank."

"I love when we prank people," Shanice giggled. "So what's the plan?"

"The talking drum uses a drum stick called a curved drumstick. The curved shape helps make the 'talking' sounds. The tip of this curved drumstick can be taken off. So, we will take the tip of the drumstick off and put a special gas inside that will be released when we beat the drum."

"This sounds gooooood," Shanice said. "So, what happens when this gas is released?"

"Everyone who smells it will get a stomachache. And they won't know why because the gas doesn't have a smell or color."

"That's a great prank! I love it!" Shanice shouted.

When we got to the festival, we saw lots of bands. There were lots of people dancing to the loud music and some people were cheering for their favorite musicians.

Shanice and I took our place in line behind our band. As we started to march through the streets and play the drums, the members of our band started to get sick. The more we played the talking drums, the sicker they got. They all started to get really hot. They began to sweat and started taking off their hats and unbuttoning their uniforms.

Shanice and I were laughing because we knew that the gas that we used in the drumsticks were working. Then the band members' stomachs started to hurt, just like I'd planned. But, even though they were not feeling well, the band members kept on marching and playing because that's how good they are. Then, the next thing that happened was not supposed to happen. I couldn't believe it. I started to get sick too. My stomach hurt so badly that I couldn't keep playing. I was bent over in pain. I had to run off to the side and throw up. I wanted to run back to join the band because I wanted to be there when the band gets to the part where they stop marching and begin to dance. I knew that I did not want to miss that part, so I started to laugh. Laughing is the way to cure the sickness that is caused by the gas. After I had a good laugh, I felt much better. Laughing helped me, but the other band members still did not feel well and they did not know what they needed to do to feel better. They were starting to be useless. They began to play the wrong music. Their steps and the music were all messed up.

"This isn't funny anymore," Shanice said.

"It is funny," I said.

"No, it's not! It's time to stop this prank," Shanice shouted. That's when she yelled to get the band members' attention.

"Hey guys! I can tell you how to get rid of your stomachaches."

"No, Shanice," I said. "I'll just get everyone to laugh since it was my idea to get everyone sick in the first place."

Shanice and I knew that laughing was the only way to get rid of the sickness, so I yelled, "Hey guys! Look at me!"

Everyone looked at me and that's when I started to do clown tricks. I drank some water from my water bottle and squirted water from one of my ears. When the band members saw this, they started to laugh. I also did a really funny giggle, and this made them laugh even more.

Once everyone started to laugh, they started to feel better. They weren't hot anymore and their stomachs didn't hurt now. So they put their hats back on, buttoned up their uniform shirts and jackets and started jamming again. Now, it was time for them to do my favorite part-the part where they dance while playing the song 'Uptown Funk' by Bruno Mars.

This was my favorite song, so I put down the talking drum, and took off my backpack. I had put my trumpet inside of my backpack before I left home. So, I took it out and joined them with the song and dancing. We were all getting down!

LESSON LEARNED: SOMETIMES A PRANK CAN BACKFIRE ON YOU. SO BE CAREFUL!

THE END

ORIGINAL ARTWORK OF : WINFRED THORPE